The Heart of a Runner

PRAISE FOR *STORYSHARES*

"One of the brightest innovators and game-changers in the education industry."
– Forbes

"Your success in applying research-validated practices to promote literacy serves as a valuable model for other organizations seeking to create evidence-based literacy programs."

- Library of Congress

"We need powerful social and educational innovation, and Storyshares is breaking new ground. The organization addresses critical problems facing our students and teachers. I am excited about the strategies it brings to the collective work of making sure every student has an equal chance in life."
– Teach For America

"Around the world, this is one of the up-and-coming trailblazers changing the landscape of literacy and education."
- International Literacy Association

"It's the perfect idea. There's really nothing like this. I mean wow, this will be a wonderful experience for young people."   - Andrea Davis Pinkney, Executive Director, Scholastic

"Reading for meaning opens opportunities for a lifetime of learning. Providing emerging readers with engaging texts that are designed to offer both challenges and support for each individual will improve their lives for years to come. Storyshares is a wonderful start."
- David Rose, Co-founder of CAST & UDL

The Heart of a Runner

Deborah Furmanski Zabek

STORYSHARES

Story Share, Inc.
New York. Boston. Philadelphia

Storyshares
Story Share, Inc.
24 N. Bryn Mawr Avenue #340
Bryn Mawr, PA 19010-3304
www.storyshares.org

Inspiring reading with a new kind of book.

Interest Level: High School
Grade Level Equivalent: 1.8

9781642611946

Book design by Storyshares

Printed in the United States of America

Storyshares Presents

1

I never was one to wake up early on a Sunday morning. My mom used to call it my lazy day. But last month, my dad challenged me. He asked me to run a 15K race with him. I'm a sucker for a challenge. And he knew it.

I told him to bring it on.

Running was never really my thing. It was my dad's. He's been running and racing for many years. He told me a 15K race was 9.3 miles. Then I panicked.

That's when Sunday mornings became my training time.

* * *

I awake extra early this morning. And I feel pumped! I'm eager to tackle this fine, spring day. I lean against Ralph, our oak tree. I need to tighten my running shoes. Years ago, my dad named this old tree Ralph. Don't ask me why. My mom wants him to chop it down. "But it's Ralph!" my dad argues.

Silly parents!

A beat up, blue sports car pulls into the driveway.

"Hey, Max! Aren't your feet full of blisters yet?"

Oh, great, I'm thinking. My best friend Franco is here to torment me. He's not into this running thing. He combs his fingers through his thick, dark hair, grinning. I roll my eyes. I know what that grin means.

A verbal sparring match.

"Don't you get blisters from tossing those pizzas?" I call out, laughing.

Franco's family owns a pizza parlor. Franco has worked there on weekends for two years. I stop in there often. He's always tossing and dropping the pizza dough.

"Not only do I toss pizzas. I eat them, too!" he jokes. He puts both hands on his belly. He calls it his starter belly. His dad has a belly like Santa Claus.

"My dad will be out soon. Come on and run with us," I tease.

"No way!" Franco chuckles. "I mean, no thanks!"

My dad trots down the driveway. Franco is backing out. My dad waves to him. He tells him to say hi to his dad.

A robin flutters out of Ralph's branches. My dad notices. He says, "Good morning, Ralph!" I tell him there's a nest with eggs in there, too.

"That's awesome," my dad says, smiling. He's a nature lover. He hands me a water bottle. We set off on our morning run.

We start running at a slow pace. I learned that from my first lesson. He also taught me to breathe from my belly. While running, we should be able to converse normally.

We'll build up my distance running. Then we'll work on speed.

During our runs, my dad and I talk a lot. We tell jokes. We talk about school. We talk about sports teams and girls. Running together has brought us closer. He seems more like a friend. Even when we don't talk, I like to run with him.

Suddenly, he turns into a dad again.

"So how are you doing with algebra?" he asks.

I should have seen that coming. I have been struggling with algebra all year.

"Lily is coming over after school tomorrow. She said she would tutor me," I reply.

My dad smiles. Then he looks at me straight in the eye. "Good, good," he says with a silly smirk. He knows my friend Lily is smart. She can ace any test a teacher could throw at her. She's also what he calls a real cutie.

I'll admit it. I do have a little crush on her. I always check the mirror before she arrives. I worry about my hair, my breath, my arm pits. She's fifteen, a year younger than me. She's pretty and popular.

"Hmm, good, good," I say right back to him.

It's been a good run today. We turn back into our driveway. My dad pats me on the shoulder as we part ways. My mom waits for him at the front door. For a moment, I watch the robin. It's pecking at its nest.

I decide I like Sunday mornings, after all.

2

My classes all seemed longer today. I couldn't wait to see Lily after school.

Deep down, I hoped she felt that way, too. After dinner, my mom and dad drink iced tea. They sit on wooden chairs next to Ralph. They seem happy there, together. My dad has even carved their names in Ralph's trunk: Dylan and Mary Parker.

Suddenly, my heart jumps. I hear Lily's voice! I peek through the kitchen curtain. She's out there saying hi to them. She's also carrying an armload of books.

I hope I have time to check the mirror!

But Lily knocks on the door before I'm ready. And that startles me! Then I trip over the rug in the hall. She must think I'm a total goof.

"Hey, Lily!" I say. "Is it tutor time, already?"

Tutor time? Did I really say that? She laughs, but in a nice way. She's sweet like that.

"Where can I set these books?" she asks, smiling. She has the cutest dimples in her cheeks.

"Oh, let me get them for you!" I offer, eagerly.

I'm trying so hard to be a gentleman. Then I plop them smack down on the kitchen table. Thump! She winces, but just a little. I offer her a chair. She sits in it. She pulls another chair next to hers. "Sit here," she says.

We talk a little before we study. I get lost in her deep blue eyes. Her brown hair falls softly over her shoulders.

I wonder what she's thinking about me. Sometimes, girls kind of scare me. I don't really know how to talk to them. But, I think that I dress cool. I work out at the gym. And people tell me I have a cute smile.

Lily pulls a book from the pile. She hands me a pencil and a worksheet. "Let's get started, hon," she says, sweetly.

She called me hon! YES!

My dad comes into the kitchen. He's wearing his running shoes. He grabs a water bottle. Then he winks at us.

"I'm going for a short run, kids. I'll see you later."

I know what he is doing. He is giving us some privacy. He's cool like that.

"Don't get lost, Dad," I say, joking.

The kitchen door closes behind him. I hear him trot down the porch steps.

This is my chance. So I say it.

"Now where were we, hon?"

3

Studying with Lily is great. And sitting close to her is great, too. Under the table, I feel our knees touch. Suddenly, the phone rings in the living room. I don't want to move an inch. Luckily, my dear mom comes to the rescue. "I'll get that, Max." I hear her pick up the phone. "Hello. Who is this? An accident? Dylan? No!"

I can hear her voice rise. And it seems all high-pitched. Something is very wrong. My heart starts to pound. "Mom, what's going on?" I call out to her.

She rushes into the kitchen. She's holding her head with both hands. Her eyes are filled with tears. "Your dad was just hit by a car!" she cries. "They've taken him to St. Luke's!"

"Oh, my God!" I shout out to her. "Is he going to be okay?"

"That's all I know, Max! I'm sorry!" she cries. "We need to get to the hospital right away!"

My head is spinning. This can't be happening! My mom, Lily and I rush out the door, panicking. Lily grabs my hand. She whispers, "I'm going with you."

We all hop in my mom's car. Three doors slam at once. I ask my mom if she's okay to drive. She nods. Her lips are clenched. In a daze, we ride to St. Luke's Hospital.

The emergency room is like a beehive. Nervous people are buzzing all around. A nurse tells us to be seated. But we can't seem to settle down. Across the room, my mom is pacing. She doesn't even look like herself. Doctors are being paged on an intercom. Why doesn't a doctor come out?

"Try not to worry, Max," Lily says to me, quietly. She looks afraid. She's holding onto my arm. But her eyes tell me that she's here for me.

"Thank you for being here," I say to her.

Suddenly, three doctors rush out of an examining room. They are talking amongst themselves. One of them shakes his head. Then he stops to look around. "Is someone here for Dylan Parker?" he asks.

I feel like I've been hit by lightening. I step forward, unsteadily. My mom clutches my arm for support.

"Where is Dylan? How is he? Can we see him now?" My mom chokes out her words.

The doctor doesn't have to say a word. I can tell by the look on his face. The news is not good. Gently, he pulls my mom and I aside. "I'm very sorry to have to tell you this," he says. "Dylan's injuries are critical. We've done all we can do for him."

Shaking, my mom covers her mouth with her hand. "Is he . . . will he . . . ?"

The doctor steps slowly away from us. He reaches for a door behind him. He opens it. He waves us in. "You can see him now, Mrs. Parker."

"Oh, Dylan!" My mom cries out loud.

The man on the gurney is so still. His face is swollen. It's covered with bloody bandages. There are monitors hooked up to him, beeping. At least he is still alive.

"Dad," my voice cracks. My knees are shaking. "Can you hear me?"

His hand twitches slightly. My mom grabs on to it. "I think he's trying to say something," she says, softly.

His lips barely move. His words come out strained. "Mary, Max. I love you both." His breathing is labored. I hear him struggle for every breath.

I brace myself for the worst.

Beep, beep, beep, skip, beep, beep, skip.

The monitors set off an alarm down the hall. I'm terrified.

My father gasps. His eyes are now locked on me.

"Don't . . . stop . . . running," he whispers, painfully.

All at once, the lines on the monitors go flat.

Beeeeeeeeeeep . . .

4

It's been three weeks since the accident. And I still can't believe my dad is gone. Grief and anger are getting the best of me. I struggle every day to be strong. But I need to stay strong. For myself. And for my mom.

"Earth to Max," I hear a voice summon. Lily is sitting next to me. We're at Franco's pizza parlor. She's holding my hand. She's been doing that a lot lately. Honestly, I don't know what I would do without her now. "You haven't even taken a bite of your pizza," she says, concerned.

"I'm not very hungry, Lily. But it feels good to be out again on a Saturday night." Then I look into her puppy dog eyes. They make me smile. So she smiles back. "I like the scenery here, too," I say.

She's worried about me. I know. But there is really nothing anyone can do to help.

Suddenly, someone comes up behind me. Chubby arms wrap me in a big bear hug. A dusting of flour falls on my shirt.

"I've missed you, man!" Franco says, cheerfully. "And good news! My dad says your pizza is on him tonight."

"Thank you, buddy," I say to him. Then I see him reach for a newspaper behind him.

"Did you see the newspaper today? There's an article about your dad. It says he was a real hero," Franco says.

I snatch the newspaper from his hand. "Let me see that," I say, curiously.

Franco and Lily sit quietly. They give me some time to read the article. I can tell they both know what it says.

It says the girl who hit my dad was texting. Her car hit my dad from behind. Now, the town is making a strict new law. They're cracking down on texting and driving.

"So, big deal," I say a little too loudly. Then I slam down the newspaper in front of my friends. Lily and Franco flinch. I say, "This stupid law is a little too late!"

"Shhhhh, Max," Franco says. He taps the article with his finger. "Keep reading."

Again, I pick up the newspaper. I read a little bit more. It also says my dad was an organ donor. He probably saved many lives. "I know about the donated organs," I say, sadly. "We talked about things like this while we ran."

I squeeze my eyes shut. I fight back the tears. But knowing this does nothing to ease my pain. The article goes on. It says that my dad was an avid runner. There's a list of the races he ran. My friends sit tight. They see my hands shake. I read through the last few lines. I see my name now. It says my dad was training me to run a 15K. I take in a long, deep breath. I let it out. Slowly, I fold up the newspaper. Then I crinkle it up and toss it away. I shake my head. I cover my face with my hands.

"Maybe it would help to start running again," Franco suggests, cautiously. Lily nods her head to agree.

"I can't run. I won't run. That was my dad's thing. Not mine!" I say, firmly.

A man at the next table is listening. Franco and I notice him at the same time.

"But, Max. Your dad was a runner. He wanted you to run, too," Franco urges.

"Shut up, Franco! I don't want to talk about this!"

My temper is quickly rising. I'm trying hard not to lose it.

The man at the next table is still listening. Franco looks at him, again. Then Franco takes a chance. He asks the man if he agrees with him.

The man tries to help. He tells me I should run again. He says it's a good idea. Suddenly, I don't know what is happening to me. My head feels like it might explode. I stand up, angrily. My chair falls over behind me. It hits the floor with a loud bang. I look at Lily. She's crying. I look at Franco. He's backing away. I want to yell at my friends. But I can't. Then I look at the man. He's standing up. He's putting his hand out.

So I lash out at him. "You don't know me at all, sir! You have no right to tell me what to do!" I yell. "I wish you'd all just leave me alone!" I storm out of the restaurant in a bitter rage. I bump into a waitress along the way. The night air hits me hard. Like a cold fist. Then the tears flow. They pour down my cheeks like a waterfall. My bottled up grief finally explodes.

There is an empty alley behind the restaurant. I walk into it to be alone. Sobbing, I cry out to the night sky.

"How can I run without my dad?"

5

Morning comes. But I stay in bed. The clock on my desk says ten o'clock. I flip over my pillow. Then I punch it. My eyes still burn from last night.

"Hey, sleepyhead! How about some breakfast?" My mom calls to me from my bedroom door.

Oh, no. I think, just go away. I'm not ready to face another day. I clear my throat. I bury my head in my pillow.

"Thanks, Mom. But I think I'll wait."

I feel ashamed, and embarrassed. Why did I blow up in front of my friends? They must be mad. I'm mad at myself! It's not like me to act this way.

'I'll be in the kitchen if you need me," my mom says. By her tone, I can tell that she's worried. She always knows when something is wrong. But she gives me some space. She's good like that. That's why I love her so much.

I roll over in my bed. I close my eyes again. I can't get Lily and Franco off my mind.

I'm such a jerk! Then I think . . .how can I ever face them again?

Suddenly, I hear a beep on my cell phone. It's on the desk, right next to my clock. I shuffle over to it. Then I sit down. There are six text messages waiting to be read.

I open the first message. It's from Franco. I brace myself for what it might say. Then I read:

"Hey Max, Are you okay? Call me. And call me, soon. Or I might have to hit you with some pizza dough!"

Good old Franco. I needed that. His message even makes me smile. Then I see five more messages. And they are all from Lily! My heart pounds as I start to read:

"Please call me as soon as you get this!"

"Please call me as soon as you get this!!!"

"Please call me as soon as you get this!!!!!"

"Please call me as soon as you get this!!!!!!!"

"Please call me as soon as you get this!!!!!!!!!"

A ray of sunlight peeks through my window. I pull back the curtain all the way. It's a beautiful day. Then I walk into the kitchen, smiling. My mom looks at me with curious eyes. I kiss her on the cheek. That makes her smile.

"I'm ready for some breakfast now," I say to her. "I'm starved!"

The Heart of a Runner

6

Some days I feel like a lucky guy. I have a great mom, a nice home, and terrific friends. Life is good, for the most part.

"So how were your classes today?" Franco asks, opening his car door.

It's the first day of the fall semester. After the last bell, Franco drives Lily and I home from school. I open the back door for Lily. She slides in. I slide in next to her.

"So far, so good, " I say, honestly.

"This should be a good year for us. We're seniors now," Franco beams. "Next year, college. Woohoo!"

Lily slaps the back of Franco's seat, jokingly. "Speak for yourself, Franco. I still have two more years," she says. The three of us laugh. We talk about our new teachers and our schedules.

The drive home is short. My house is not far from school. So Franco drops me off first. Franco pulls into the driveway. There's a strange car parked in front of the garage. "Did your mom get a new car?" Franco asks, curiously.

"Nope," I say. "I have no idea who that is. But I'll find out soon enough!" Franco pulls out of the driveway. He honks the horn three times. Lily moves next to the window. She waves to me.

I throw my backpack over my shoulder. I walk past the strange car. I check it out. I'm eager to see who's visiting my mom.

"I'm glad you're home, Max," my mom calls out. "There's someone here. I'd like you to meet him."

A man is sitting at the kitchen table. All I can see is his back. There are some papers on the table in front of him. And he's holding another one in his hand. The man stands up. He turns around to shake my hand. He looks familiar.

"My name is Jackson Wells. It's nice to finally meet you, Max," he says. I look puzzled. So the man smiles at me. Then his expression becomes more serious. "Sit down. I'll explain who I am and why I'm here," he says. He tells me he is a runner. And he's the president of a local running club. A lot of his club members knew my dad. I listen to him speak. Even his voice has a familiar tone. "Your dad was a good man," he says. "He was training you to run a 15K. I'm sorry you didn't get to run it with him."

I don't know what to say to him. And why does he look so familiar? Jackson Wells hands me the paper that he's holding. It's an entry form for a race. I look at the papers on the table. They are running maps. Then he chooses his words, carefully. "I'd like to honor your father, Max. His death really touched my heart. But I need you to help me," he says.

"Are you asking me to run this race with you?" I ask. I toss the entry form on the table. I look at him straight in the eye.

"It's not a race, Max. It's a marathon. A marathon is 26.2 miles. This is the perfect tribute to your dad."

Suddenly, I know who this man is. But I still don't know why this would matter to him. "You're the man from Franco's pizza parlor! You sat at the table next to mine! Why are you still pushing me?" I cry out, angrily.

I look at my mom. She brushes a tear away from her eye. Then she grabs both of my hands. "I think you should do this, Max. It would be good for you," she says, softly. Then she pauses. She wants to say something more. But she hesitates. "Do... you remember your father's last words?" she asks, gently.

The awful night of his death still haunts me. I remember his last words well. Painfully, I choke out my dad's last words. "He said . . . 'Don't . . . stop . . . running'."

Jackson Wells puts his hand on my shoulder. I shrug it off. "Just think about this, Max. You don't have to decide today," he says. He gathers up his papers. He walks quietly to the kitchen door. The door closes behind him. I hear his car engine start. He begins to back out.

Then suddenly, I jump up from my chair. "Mr. Wells! Wait!" I holler out to him. He stops his car at the end of the driveway. I see him waiting at the wheel. "Okay!" I yell to him. "Let's... do this!"

Jackson Wells nods, satisfied. With a wink, he tells me he'll be in touch. Then he drives away.

A sudden breeze stirs my mom's wind chimes. They tinkle softly in the crisp autumn air.

I walk over toward Ralph. I sit down next to him in my dad's chair. My mom follows me. She sits in her chair. We both look up. We see a leaf fall from one of Ralph's branches. It drops gently into my lap like a tear.

I bite my lip. "I'm sorry, Ralph," I say to him. "I know you miss my dad, too."

7

Jackson Wells returned the following weekend. We filled out the entry forms. Our marathon is now set for the spring.

"This is an awesome trail, Mr. Wells," I say to him. "It was one of my dad's favorites, too."

Mr. Wells is running beside me. We're running on one of the nature trails. This one is paved. It's lined with tall trees. And there's a peaceful river that runs alongside it.

Mr. Wells glances around. He is also enjoying the scenic trail. "We've been running together for two months," he says, smiling. "Why don't you just call me, Jack!"

"Okay, Mr. Wells," I say. "Oops, I mean, Jack." I like running with Jack. And I've learned a lot of new things from him. I've learned about diet, hydration and running gear. He bought me a special belt. It holds my water bottle. We carry water or a sports drink to stay hydrated. He also has a strict running plan. And he pushes me when he has to. I've learned to respect that.

Training for a marathon is tough. He keeps me focused on our main goal: The finish line.

Jack and I have become good friends. We talk a lot while we run. But I've noticed something. Jack never mentions his family. I'm curious.

"Do you have a family, Jack? Do you have any children?" I ask.

Jack doesn't answer right away. He continues to run. I can tell that he's thinking. He hesitates. But then he speaks. "I have a wife. We've been married for many years. I also have a son," he replies.

That seems odd. Why hasn't Jack mentioned his son before?

"Does your son run, too?" I ask, curiously. Jack slows down the running pace. I can see that my question has affected him.

"Kyle was born with a heart defect," he explains. "He's now a grown man. About your mom's age. The heart defect made him weak. He's spent many years in a wheel chair."

"I'm sorry to hear that," I say to him. "I'd like to meet him some day."

"You will," Jack says. "I promise you."

Suddenly, Jacks speeds up the running pace. So I take the hint. I drop the subject. Then he starts to run faster. And then faster yet! He turns to me, laughing.

"Come on, Max!" he says. He's challenging me to race with him! We both start to run at full speed. We run hard until we're nearly out of breath. We're having fun! We see a bench on the trail up ahead. We reach it at the same time. Then we collapse on it. We sit for a moment to catch our breath. Then Jack pulls out his running watch. He shakes his head. Then he winks at me.

"It's almost dinnertime," he says, standing up again. "I'll race you home."

8

It's the day before the marathon. So today is a day of rest. The long months of training are behind me now. It's a good day to spend with some friends.

"You go in first, Max!" Lily says to me, giggling. She's almost pushing me through the door of Franco's pizza parlor. I suspect that something is going on.

"Okay, okay!" I say, giving up.

Suddenly, Franco opens the heavy door from inside. He gives me one of his sneaky grins. I glance around. I see all my friends there. Then I notice a large banner. It's strung across the back wall. It says, "Good Luck, Max!"

"Surprise!" they all yell at once. Franco's father comes out of the kitchen. He's carrying a pizza on a tray. He makes room for it on a buffet table.

He steps back. Then he waves his arms. "Come on everyone! Let's eat!" he says.

All my best friends are here. I am happy to see them. I missed seeing them during the months I was training. One by one, my friends come over to wish me luck. We catch up a little. We share some laughs. Then we head to the buffet table.

"Excuse me, please!" Franco says to the gang. Then he throws his chubby arm over my shoulder. He drags me to the head of the buffet line. "Let's let our running star go first!" he says.

"You guys are too much," I say to them, feeling humbled. "I couldn't ask for better friends."

The food on the table all looks good to me. I wish I could eat it all. But I'm a runner now. So I stick to the foods on my running plan.

Lily calls to me from a booth in the corner. She motions for me to sit next to her. So I carry my plate to her table. "How do you like Franco's surprise?" she asks. "He's been planning this for a week!"

I look down at my plate of food. I look around at my friends and the good luck banner. I see the excitement in Lily's eyes. Suddenly, I'm feeling some pre-race jitters. "The party is great, Lily. But I'm starting to feel a little nervous," I say, honestly.

Lily looks at me with her puppy dog eyes. Then her wide smile makes her dimples show. "I know you can do this, Max," she whispers quietly. Then she reaches for my hand. "You've worked so hard. Stop worrying."

I'm trying so hard to stay positive. But the fear of failure is too strong. "I need to do well tomorrow. There are so many people involved. I don't want to let anyone down," I confess.

For a moment, Lily sits quietly. She tries to find the right words to say.

Then a burst of laughter comes from another table. Lily and I turn our heads. Across the room, Franco is tossing some pizza dough. Then everyone starts to clap for him. He throws the pizza dough high in the air. He spins it around and around. Then he tosses it high in the air again.

He doesn't drop it today. That makes me smile.

Suddenly, I feel a burst of confidence. Then I turn to Lily. I squeeze her hand. "I'm feeling better now," I assure her. "And I'm going to run this marathon . . . for my dad."

9

I've never seen such a crowd in my life. There are runners and spectators everywhere. Then I see what I'm looking for. Our starting corral. So I weave my way to where I belong.

"Hey, Max! Over here!" It's Jack's voice. I hear him calling me from somewhere in the crowd. Then I see him waiting for me by our starting corral. He's waving his arms and a hat to get my attention.

I wave back. I want him to know that I see him there.

"This is it, Max! This is what we've been training for!" he shouts as I approach him.

When I reach him, I throw my arms around him. He hugs me back. Then he checks my runner's bib and all my running gear. We jog in place to loosen our leg muscles. Then we shake hands with a few other runners. We stand shoulder to shoulder with them in the crowded corral. A rock band is playing on the sideline. And from up ahead, we can hear an announcer saying something. It's hard to hear him above the voices in the crowd. Suddenly, we hear a pistol shot. The runners slowly begin to move forward. The starting corral thins out ahead of us. Jack and I jog up to the official starting line.

"Remember to start out slow, Max," Jack reminds me. "Don't get caught up in all this excitement. We need to save our energy for the last few miles."

Jack is right. The lively music has revved up my energy level. And the cheers from the spectators ring in my ears. I'm lucky to have him here. I watch some of the other runners make this mistake.

The first few miles go by quickly. There are smiling faces and bandstands along the way. Spectators clap as we approach them. Everyone shouts to cheer us on.

A member of Jack's running club calls from the sideline. Jack waves to him to say hi. "Great job, Jack! Keep up the good work!" he calls out to him.

By the ten mile mark, my legs begin to grow weary. But I draw more strength from the music and the crowds. Some of the spectators are holding up signs. Reading them helps to pass the time.

"Check out some of these signs, Jack! I see some real funny ones up ahead!" I say. Then I read them aloud as we run by.

"May the course be with you!"

"Your shoe laces are untied!"

"Run Forrest Run!" Jack laughs. Then he points out another sign. He reads it aloud. "The end is near!"

"Ha ha," I say to him. "Don't we wish! We still have at least ten miles to go!"

Jack and I continue to run. It helps that we can run side by side. But the crowds are thinning out. And we're both getting tired. And the hardest miles of the race are still ahead. Suddenly, I hear a siren. I turn my head to see what's going on. I see a runner is down on the sideline. There is a crowd of people gathering around.

"I sure hope that runner is okay," I say to Jack. Then I look over for him. But he's not there.

I turn my head around. I see Jack lagging behind.

He doesn't look right. His footwork is all wrong. He looks like he is running through thick mud.

"Hey, Jack! Are you all right?" I ask, slowing down.

He waves a hand at me. He's motioning for me to go on ahead. "I'll be fine, Max. Just go ahead," he says.

I jog in place while Jack catches up to me. I don't like the strange look on his face.

10

Jack slows down to a walking pace. He looks dazed. I think he might have "hit the wall".

"Hitting the wall" is a term used by marathon runners. It happens at around twenty miles. That's when a body has used up all its energy reserves. It causes confusion, weakness, and severe pain.

The other runners are weaving around us now. So I pull Jack to the sideline to keep him safe.

"Let's get another sports drink in you, Jack," I say to him. I unhook a bottle from his running belt. He takes a few sips. Then he shakes his head.

"I'm probably getting too old for this," he says, soberly. "Sometimes I forget that I'm an old man."

"Don't say that, Jack. I think you've just hit the wall. Now, drink! We'll get through this," I say.

It's important for Jack to drink the sports drink. It's full of vitamins and some sugar. It's also important for him to clear his mind. To get rid of his negative thoughts. He needs to focus. He needs me to push him now. Like he's pushed me.

"I don't want to hold you back," he says. "I'll be okay. Just go!"

"That's not going to happen, Jack! We're in this together!" I yell. "I don't care if we both finish last today! But we are going to cross that finish line!"

Jack takes a few gulps of his sports drink. Then he trots slowly back into the running lane. He grits his teeth. He pushes himself through the pain.

Slowly, he picks up the pace again. But he still needs me to help keep his mind alert.

Then I think back to one of our training runs. It was the day that I asked about his son, Kyle. Something happened to him that day. I don't know if it was good or bad. Maybe it would help if I mentioned Kyle.

"I'd like to hear more about your son," I say. Then I wait and hope for the right response. Suddenly, Jack turns to me. His eyes are glassy. And he looks . . . almost terrified. I wonder what is going through his mind. "What is it, Jack?" I ask him, gently. "What's wrong?"

Jack takes in a deep breath. He lets it out slowly. He wrings his hands. "There is something that we need to talk about," he says, nervously. "It's about Kyle. It's about you. And about your dad." Jack runs a little further. He builds up his nerve. Then he starts his long story from the beginning. "Do you remember that night at Franco's pizza parlor? The night that you were reading a newspaper?" he asks.

I nod my head, confused.

"I didn't mean to eavesdrop that night. But I couldn't help myself. The story about your dad was all too familiar," he says.

I'm still confused. I tell him to go on.

"You know that Kyle was born with a heart defect. He was a very sick man. He was getting weaker. His doctor said that he was going to die," he explains, sadly. Jack looks away. He thinks for a moment before going on. "Three weeks before you saw me at Franco's, something happened. Kyle got a phone call that changed his life. It was wonderful news for him. But sadly, the news was not good for someone else," he says. Jacks looks down. He pauses. He struggles to find the right words to say. "There'd been an accident. A runner died after being struck by a car. My wife, Kyle and I rushed to the hospital," he confesses. "That night . . . Kyle received a new heart."

Jack's words hit me like a solid blow to my chest. My legs feel wobbly. I can't speak.

"My son received a second chance at life that night," he says. I was so happy for him. But I was sad at the same time. My heart ached for the hero who'd just lost his life."

He keeps his head down. He wipes away some tears. Then he finishes. "Then three weeks later . . . that night at Franco's . . . I found myself face to face with that hero's son." Then he turns to me. His eyes search mine for some kind of acceptance. All at once, I realize why Jack had been drawn to me. We share this connection. My dad's heart still beats in his son's chest.

Still running, I stretch my arms out to him. We embrace each other in tears. Our legs keep moving forward. We keep running together toward our common goal.

Up ahead, we see the banner that says finish line. Lily, Franco and my mom are waiting behind it. They are clapping, and cheering. Lily is jumping up and down.

Jack and I take our last strides toward the finish line. We cross it. We are completely drained. We fall to our knees. There is a band playing. The crowd has grown again. There are hugs and kisses. There are pats on the back.

We all walk together toward the awards desk. We receive our medals. We shake hands with the officials. Then we move along to get away from the crowd.

Suddenly, a man steps out from the sidelines. Jack walks over to him. They share a long embrace. Jack waves me over. The man shakes my hand, firmly. Then he puts his other hand on my shoulder.

"Hello Max. It's an honor to finally meet you," he says. "I'm Jack's son, Kyle."

11

A year has passed since the marathon. It's springtime, again. I'm still a runner.And I'm proud of it. I think my dad would be proud, too.

Lily and I are sitting in the wooden chairs next to Ralph. We're watching a robin build a new nest.

"Why don't robins use the same nest every year?" Lily asks, amused.

"I'm not sure," I say. "But I've heard that they return to the same nesting area. This robin and Ralph must be good buddies."

Lily giggles. "I think you're right," she agrees.

Inside the house, the phone rings. We hear my mom answer it. We hear her laughing. Then she steps out onto the front porch.

A car pulls into the driveway. Lily and I watch as a mansteps out. He waves to us.

"See you later, kids," my mom says. Then she pauses for a second. She looks as if she's forgotten something.

"And good morning to you, Ralph," she says, smiling.

She walks up to the man. She hands him a water bottle. We watch them start walking together down the road.

When they get to the corner, they stop. They look around. My mom points toward the nature trail.

They decide to walk that way. They take a few steps.

Then together, my mom and Kyle begin a slow trot.

About The Author

Deborah Furmanski-Zabek wrote "The Heart of A Runner" in 2015 during Storyshares first annual Story of the Year contest. It quickly became part of the library's core collection, where it has been shared in classrooms all around the globe.

About The Publisher

Story Shares is a nonprofit focused on supporting the millions of teens and adults who struggle with reading by creating a new shelf in the library specifically for them. The ever-growing collection features content that is compelling and culturally relevant for teens and adults, yet still readable at a range of lower reading levels.

Story Shares generates content by engaging deeply with writers, bringing together a community to create this new kind of book. With more intriguing and approachable stories to choose from, the teens and adults who have fallen behind are improving their skills and beginning to discover the joy of reading. For more information, visit storyshares.org.

Easy to Read. Hard to Put Down.

www.ingramcontent.com/pod-product-compliance
Lightning Source LLC
Chambersburg PA
CBHW071225170626
46809CB00005BA/1933